# ACTION MAN

## JUNGLE MISSION

First published in Great Britain 2001
This edition published in 2003
by Egmont Books Limited
239 Kensington High Street, London W8 6SA
*Jungle Mission* originally published as *Rumble in the Jungle*
by Panini Comics, a division of Panini UK Ltd

ISBN  1 4052 0769 8

1 3 5 7 9 10 8 6 4 2

Printed and bound in China

# EGMONT

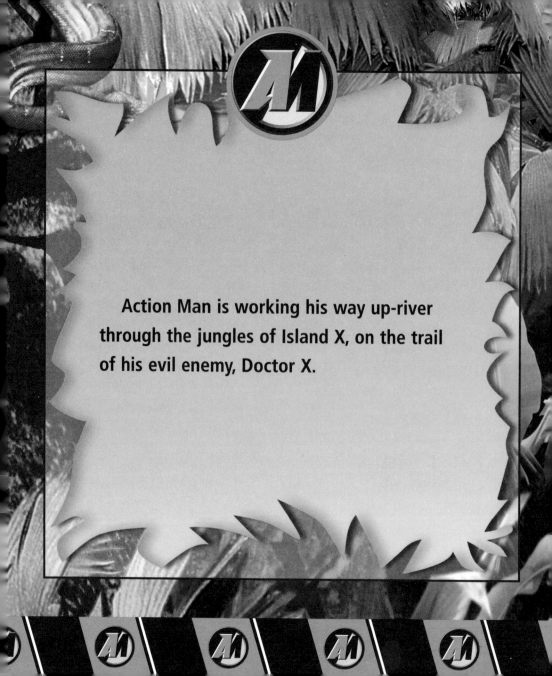

Action Man is working his way up-river through the jungles of Island X, on the trail of his evil enemy, Doctor X.

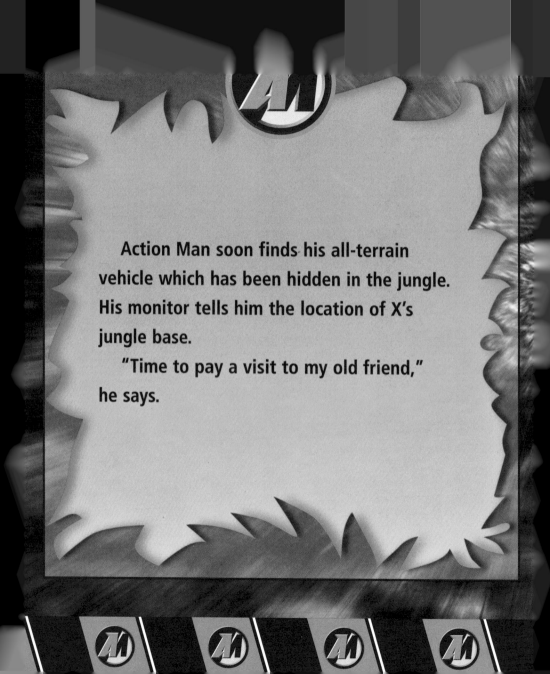

Action Man soon finds his all-terrain vehicle which has been hidden in the jungle. His monitor tells him the location of X's jungle base.

"Time to pay a visit to my old friend," he says.

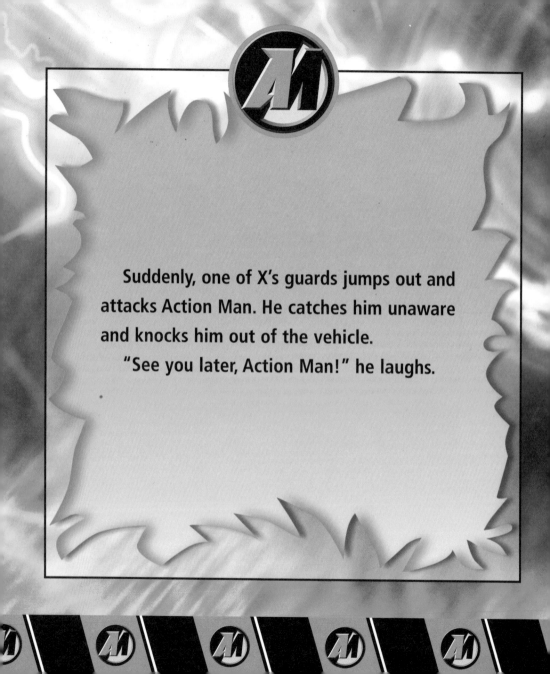

Suddenly, one of X's guards jumps out and attacks Action Man. He catches him unaware and knocks him out of the vehicle.

"See you later, Action Man!" he laughs.

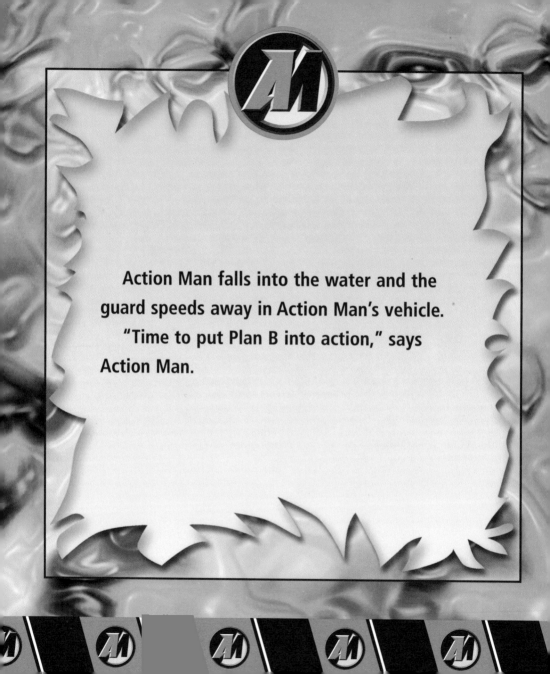

Action Man falls into the water and the guard speeds away in Action Man's vehicle. "Time to put Plan B into action," says Action Man.

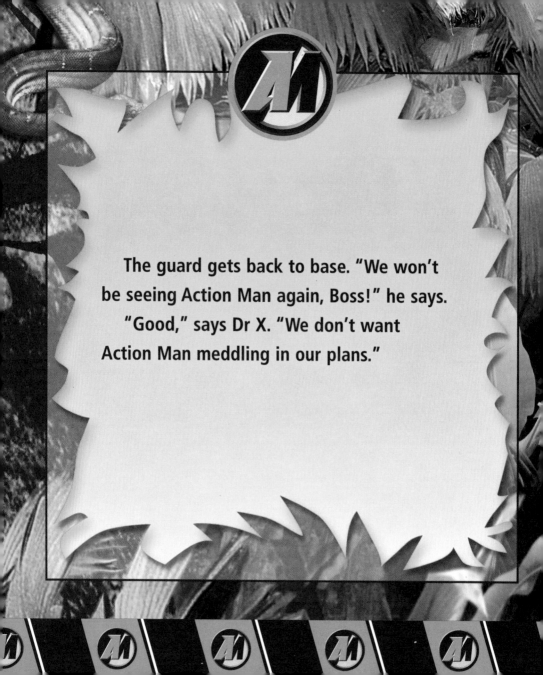

The guard gets back to base. "We won't
be seeing Action Man again, Boss!" he says.
"Good," says Dr X. "We don't want
Action Man meddling in our plans."

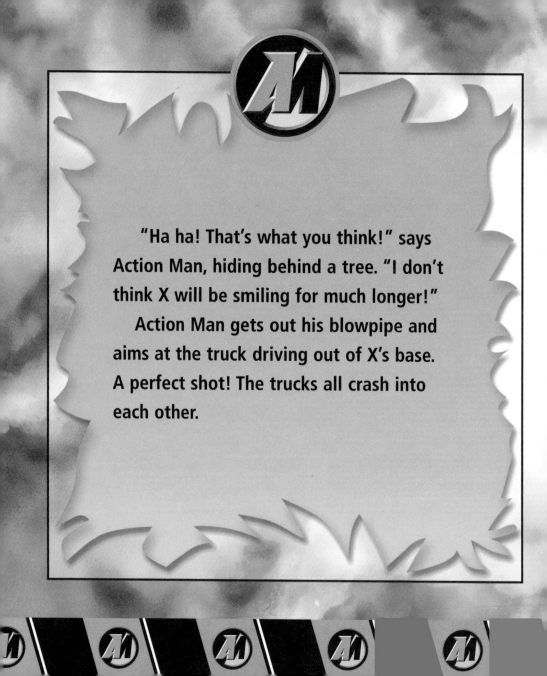

"Ha ha! That's what you think!" says Action Man, hiding behind a tree. "I don't think X will be smiling for much longer!"

Action Man gets out his blowpipe and aims at the truck driving out of X's base. A perfect shot! The trucks all crash into each other.

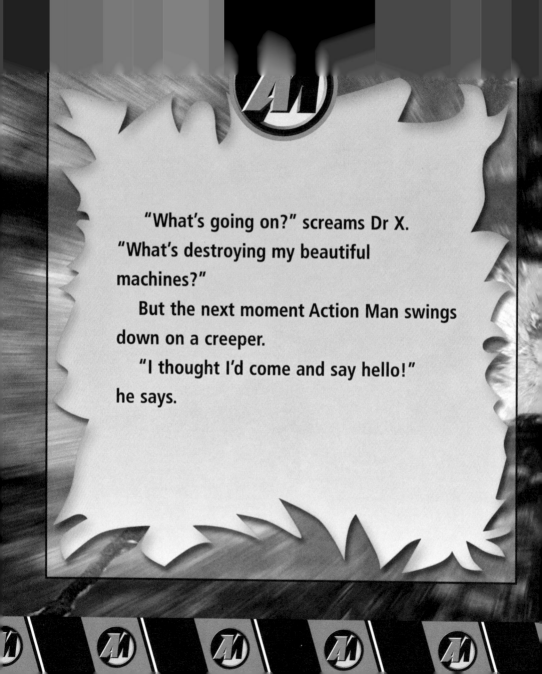

"What's going on?" screams Dr X. "What's destroying my beautiful machines?"

But the next moment Action Man swings down on a creeper.

"I thought I'd come and say hello!" he says.

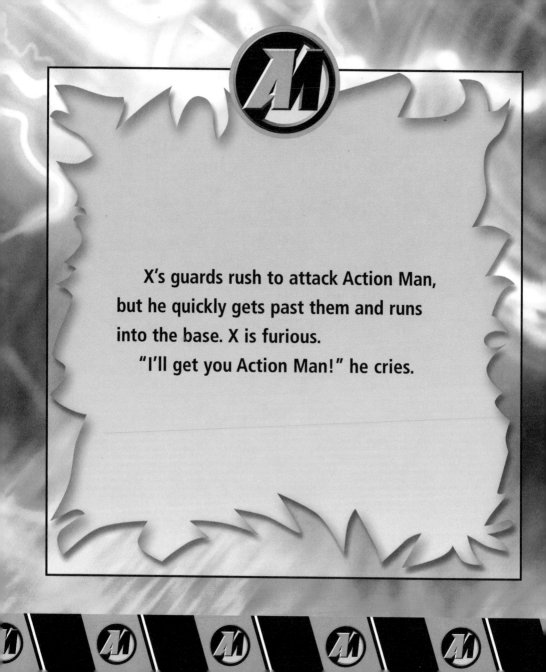

X's guards rush to attack Action Man, but he quickly gets past them and runs into the base. X is furious.

"I'll get you Action Man!" he cries.

Dr X chases after Action Man and grabs him from behind. Action Man quickly leaps out of the way and X's hand smashes through the wall. Suddenly water blasts through the hole, taking X with it!

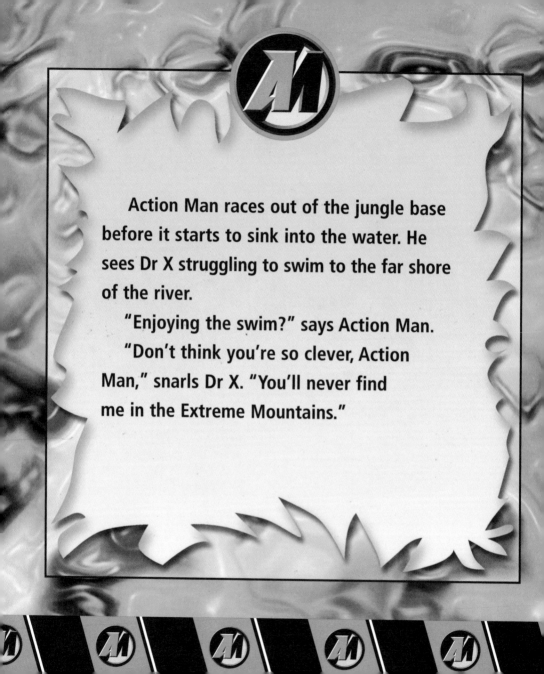

Action Man races out of the jungle base before it starts to sink into the water. He sees Dr X struggling to swim to the far shore of the river.

"Enjoying the swim?" says Action Man.

"Don't think you're so clever, Action Man," snarls Dr X. "You'll never find me in the Extreme Mountains."